WITHDRAWN

Ripple Effect

Ripple Effect

SYLVIA TAEKEMA

ORCA BOOK PUBLISHERS

Library and Archives Canada Cataloguing in Publication

Taekema, Sylvia, 1964–, author
Ripple effect / Sylvia Taekema.

Issued in print and electronic formats.
ISBN 978-1-4598-0872-0 (pbk.).—ISBN 978-1-4598-0873-7 (pdf).—
ISBN 978-1-4598-0874-4 (epub)

I. Title.
PS8639.A25R56 2015   jc813'.6   C2015-901704-1
C2015-901705-X

First published in the United States, 2015
Library of Congress Control Number: 2015935511

Summary: Dana's relationship with her best friend is put to the test when Janelle
is injured in a summer biking accident.

*Orca Book Publishers is dedicated to preserving the environment and
has printed this book on Forest Stewardship Council® certified paper.*

Orca Book Publishers gratefully acknowledges the support for its publishing programs
provided by the following agencies: the Government of Canada through the Canada Book
Fund and the Canada Council for the Arts, and the Province of British Columbia
through the BC Arts Council and the Book Publishing Tax Credit.

Cover design by Teresa Bubela
Cover image by Getty Images
Author photo by Denise Blommestyn

ORCA BOOK PUBLISHERS
www.orcabook.com

Printed and bound in Canada.

18 17 16 15 • 4 3 2 1

For my daughters

One

"JANELLE IS YOUR best friend, Dana. We should go."

Dana stood at the bottom of the stairs. She looked over at her dad, who was waiting in the hallway, truck keys in hand.

"I went already, with Grandpa, remember?"

"I know. But that was weeks ago. The truck's all fixed now and—"

"For now," Dana said with a half smile. "It's such a long way, Dad. I think we'd better take it easy on that old truck. You need it for work."

After being laid off from the factory all winter, Dana's dad had started his own lawn-care business back in April. He'd been so busy all summer he didn't have time to take Dana to the library or the swimming pool, let alone drive to the children's hospital an hour away to see Janelle. Dana's mother didn't have a car. She was intense about doing her part to save the environment and always took the bus to work. As a result, Dana and her brother, Dale, walked everywhere or took their bikes.

When Dana's grandfather had come to visit for a week at the end of July, he'd taken her up to the hospital in his little rental car. He'd helped her find the right room. Janelle's mom and dad and aunt and uncle were there, everyone talking in whispers. Nelly was pale. Her entire left leg was set in a cast and rested in a harness suspended above the bed. It looked uncomfortable. It also looked like it would be really hard for Janelle to move around, but maybe that didn't matter because she was so very, very still. Her eyes were closed. Dana felt ill. Her heart thumped oddly. She wiped her sweaty hands on her shorts and took a deep breath. She was still trying to get up the courage to walk over to the bed when a nurse had come in and shooed everyone out. "Too many visitors," she said. "This girl needs to rest."

Dana's grandfather had spoken with Janelle's parents in the hallway outside the room for a few minutes while Dana sat on a bench. Then he took her out for a milkshake, but she didn't really taste it. He told her all kinds of funny stories from his travels, but she only half heard them. "I know you're disappointed about not being able to visit with your friend," her grandpa had said, resting a hand on her shoulder. Dana didn't tell him that she had actually felt relieved.

Over the next few weeks, Dana had tried a few times to call Janelle's room. Dana's mother had gotten the number for her. The first time she called, the phone just rang and rang, and that scared her. Why didn't Janelle answer? Had something bad happened? It wasn't like she could go anywhere with her leg the way it was. The second time, a nurse answered and said Janelle was with a physiotherapist. The third time, Janelle's dad answered and said she was down at X-ray. He asked if Dana could call back in a half hour or so. "Sure," Dana had said. But she didn't. She just…didn't.

All through the summer, Dana's mother had kept asking her if she was all right.

"I'm fine. Why wouldn't I be?"

"I mean, with what happened to Janelle and everything."

Dana was puzzled. "It didn't happen to me, Mom."

"It did, in a sense. These things touch people in different ways."

Dana shrugged. She didn't understand what her mom was getting at. "I'm okay." She knew everything would be fine again once Janelle was home.

Dana's dad kept saying things like "Next week doesn't look so bad," or "I think I can be caught up in a few more days." But it rained enough to keep the grass green and growing, and the weeds seemed to do double time in the heat. Then the truck broke down. It stayed in the shop for a whole week while Dana's dad rescheduled with his customers and worked to catch up on his bookkeeping at the kitchen table. But now the truck was fixed. And even though he was swamped with jobs again,

Dana's dad insisted he would take the afternoon off so that Dana could visit Janelle.

"Dana, when your friend is in the hospital—"

"I hate hospitals, Dad," Dana cut in. "They smell funny. And I hate all those tubes and machines and beeping noises. The whole place makes *me* feel sick. I'm not like Mom. I would make a terrible nurse." She shuddered and sat down on the bottom stair.

Her dad sighed. "No one's asking you to be a nurse, Dana."

"Dad, Nelly knows me. She knows I think hospitals are creepy. Remember when Dale broke his wrist in the basketball game last winter and you and Mom and I brought him to Emergency? How you had to call Mrs. Murphy and Janelle to come get me because I was starting to look like more of a patient than Dale was?"

Her father laughed. "I remember."

"And Janelle knows all about our old truck too. She won't care. She'll understand."

Her father shook his head. "I hope you're right." He took off his good jacket and hung it back in the closet. Then he took his work jacket off the hook by the door and tossed it over his shoulder.

"C'mon, Dad." Dana tried to make her voice sound light. "Chances are, we'd drive all the way down there and not even see her because she'd be busy with a physiotherapist or something. She's working really hard so she can come home. And Mrs. Murphy told Mom they're hoping Janelle will be at school when it starts next week. I've called a bunch of times, and I've been writing to her, you know, to keep her spirits up and keep her up-to-date."

"Yeah?"

"Yeah. Of course. She's my best friend, Dad."

"I know." He ran a hand through his wavy hair and then turned toward the door. "I guess I'll see you at supper then."

"Okay. I'll start packing my stuff for the weekend."

Dana turned around and went back upstairs to her room. She heard her dad drive away in the truck, and she let out a long, slow breath. Dana knew she should visit her friend, but she really hated hospitals and seeing Janelle there was just—sad. She wasn't supposed to be there. It wasn't the same. *She* wasn't the same. Where was the smiling, energetic Nelly she knew?

Dana pulled some shorts and her swimsuit out of a drawer and stuffed them into her duffel bag. She rolled up a beach towel and a sweater and shoved those in as well. She was going camping for the weekend with her aunt Sandy. They went every summer just before school started. She pulled her sleeping bag out of her closet and then sat down on her bed and sighed. She felt angry with herself, but she also felt bad for not telling her dad the truth. She had meant to write to Janelle. She'd started more than once. She'd pulled out several sheets of the pink paper that she'd gotten as a birthday gift a few years ago. They were heart-shaped and smelled like bubble gum. But she couldn't send that to Janelle at the hospital. Too cheery. And the regular lined paper she'd found in her desk drawer felt too boring. Like she was doing a school project.

Dana didn't know what to say in the letter either. Janelle had been in a terrible accident.

She'd taken her bike to pick up a couple of things from the grocery store for her mom. While she was crossing the street on her way home, a car missed the red light completely but hit Nelly straight on. She'd been at the children's hospital for six weeks already. When Mrs. Murphy had first called to tell Dana's mother the news, she was crying. She wasn't even sure Janelle would make it. There were no visitors allowed then. Now everyone was sure she would be all right, but they didn't know how her leg would heal.

What was Dana supposed to write after Janelle had been through something like that? Should she keep her up-to-date on summer soccer? She'd just be reminding her of all the games she couldn't play. Should she tell her they'd put in a new diving board at the pool? She'd just be reminding her that she couldn't swim. Should she tell her she'd worked at Emerald Acres for two weeks picking beans? She'd just be reminding her of all the money she didn't make, money they were both hoping to use for back-to-school stuff. She could tell her she'd finally gotten her braces two weeks ago and how annoying it was when toothbrush bristles got caught in them or how awkward it was when her lip got hung up on them, but these things seemed like nothing compared to what Janelle was going through.

Dana did want to tell Janelle how she'd used her time in the bean field to do a lot of thinking, and that she'd finally worked up the courage to tell Jason Elwood straight out that she liked him. But that wasn't something you wrote in a letter. What if someone else accidentally read it? No way. That was totally classified information. So Dana didn't write anything. But she was positive Janelle would understand. She would know Dana was thinking about her. They'd been friends for a long time.

Summer was almost over now, and they could forget about everything and move forward. School started next week, and Janelle would be there and they could start grade six at Emery Elementary as if nothing had ever happened.

Two

JANELLE WASN'T THERE. At least, she wasn't waiting for Dana at the bike racks like she'd done every other morning since kindergarten. Dana saw a few other kids from her class. She smiled at Ben, who was sitting on the curb reading a book, and waved at Charlotte, McKayla, Avery and Allie, who were playing four square. Trey was hollering and kicking a soccer ball back and forth with Greg and Tyler. That boy had the loudest voice of anyone she'd ever met. Dana slid her bike into the rack and secured her lock around the front tire. She tried to flatten her windblown hair as she jogged around the corner, lugging a backpack crammed with all her back-to-school stuff. She wished her mom understood that kids needed a ride on the first day. There was just too much to carry. And how could she hope to look even a little bit cool when she had to put an elastic band around her ankle to keep her new jeans from being chewed up by the bike chain?

"Just think what you're showing the other kids by riding your bike," her mom had said when Dana complained.

"What a good idea it is to get a ride on the first day?"

"No, you're showing them how much you care."

"Could you show me how much you care and call Dad to come give me a ride?"

"Love you, honey," her mother had said with a wink as she left for the bus stop.

Dana also wished her mom understood that there might not be time for breakfast on the first day of school.

"It's the most important meal of the day," she had said, handing Dana a box of granola. Dana had opted for peanut-butter toast instead, but it had come out burned and crunchy. She had left it in too long while deciding what to wear. Their toaster was old and didn't pop up by itself anymore, but her mother wouldn't buy a new one. "Why?" she would ask. "This one still works."

Peanut butter had stuck to the back of Dana's throat as she jammed everything into her backpack. Forget brushing her teeth. She'd barely had time to do her hair, trying desperately to pull down a couple of curls to hide the weekend's mosquito bites, only to see them spring right back up again. She had hoped to get to school before Janelle arrived, but now she was late. A group of grade-six girls stood talking outside a set of double doors. Dana didn't see Nelly anywhere. She eased into the circle.

"Hey, guys." She smiled.

"Oh, hello, Dana." It was Julia Lambert, self-appointed class queen. "We were just talking about you."

I'll bet.

"I guess it must be weird for you. Not having Janelle here, I mean."

Dana stiffened. "She's not here? Her mom said she would be out of the hospital in time."

Julia narrowed her eyes. *Was it intentional, or was her ponytail just way too tight?*

"Oh, she's home. She's just not up to being at school yet, poor thing. When I saw her last night, she was so disappointed."

"You saw her last night? I haven't seen her for—" Dana hesitated. It was too complicated to explain everything, and she didn't want Julia making a big deal of it.

"Didn't you see her or talk to her at all this weekend? Then you would have known all about it."

Dana bristled. "I was away camping this weekend, and we didn't get in until last night. We go every year before school starts. Janelle knows that. And she wouldn't miss the first day. I'm sure she'll walk in any minute."

"Oh, she won't walk. She can't. She's using a wheelchair. Didn't you know that? Didn't you visit her in the hospital?"

"Of course. But she was mostly tired and busy with physio and stuff."

Julia looked at her strangely. "I visited her every week. My mom took me down when she had her regional real-estate meetings. They don't schedule physio and stuff during visiting hours, actually. We had time for some nice long chats."

Every week? An uncomfortable thought seeped into Dana's head. She hadn't been able to talk to Janelle, but if Janelle was home, why hadn't she tried to call either? Because Dana had been away camping? Janelle must have known that. Still, doubt prickled over her like goose bumps. All summer long she'd missed her friend. What if her friend didn't miss her? She didn't have time to think about it for long. The bell rang, and everyone rushed inside.

Three

JULIA WAS RIGHT about one thing. It *was* weird without Janelle there. She and Dana had talked constantly about being in grade six and having Mr. Bartholomew as their teacher. It was going to be the best year ever. They'd been on the cross-country team for a long time already, but now they could join volleyball, basketball and soccer too. Grade six always had amazing projects hanging on the walls outside the classroom, and they did awesome science experiments. In grade five, Dana's class had played recorders for the fall talent show, but grade six put on a play every year. It was going to be great.

Dana chose a desk midway down the first row. She didn't want to be right up front, but she didn't feel like sitting in the back with Julia and the others either. She tucked her pencils and binder away but kept out her markers and the stack of bright-green, frog-shaped sticky notes she had bought. She'd had fun back-to-school shopping, but not as much fun as she would have had if she'd gone with Janelle.

She pulled off the first sticky note. Taking out a purple marker, Janelle's favorite color, Dana drew Janelle's name in big bubble letters. She would save the seat beside her until Nelly came back. Dana hoped that was soon. Very soon. As she reached over with her sticky note, Mickey Ramirez bulldozed his way down the row and threw his backpack on the desk. Dana glared at him. There was no way she was going to sit beside Mickey Ramirez. He had teased her since kindergarten.

Mickey loved making little rhymes with her name: *Dana, Dana, is a whooping crane-a. Can be such a pain-a. She is so insane-a.* The teasing had started years ago when Mickey had first learned Dana's full name. Dana Dawn Davis. All through kindergarten Mickey had called her Ding Dong Davis. And it had caught on. Kids still used the nickname in grade one. Mickey held on to it until grade two. Almost everyone seemed to have forgotten it by now, but Dana hadn't. She lived in fear of hearing it again. She'd never forgiven Mickey either. No way was he sitting that close.

Dana, Dana, your year's going down the drain-a. And it was only the first day. She had to do something.

"Mickey, that desk..."

Mickey wasn't listening. "Jason!" he called. "Hey, Jay, sit here." Mickey squeezed himself into a desk in the third row, waving his hand and pointing to where his backpack sat. Jason Elwood made his way down row two. Dana sat down. Jason Elwood? Sitting in the desk beside her? She quietly crumpled up the sticky note she'd been holding and slipped it into her desk. Janelle would understand.

Jason took a long time getting to his seat, talking with everyone along the way. He hadn't gotten a back-to-school haircut. His shirt was untucked. The knees on his jeans were scuffed, and both shoelaces were untied on his worn Nikes. And he was absolutely perfect. Dana knew she should talk to him, but what would she say? She could ask him how his summer was. That was safe. That was normal conversation for the first day of school. Finally, Jason sat down. He tossed Mickey his backpack, pulled two pencils, a pen and an eraser out of his shirt pocket and put them in the desk. At last, he looked in her direction. He pushed his dark hair out of his eyes. "Hey, Dana."

Dana tried to meet his gaze casually. His eyes were a warm green, and his face was deeply tanned except for a scar on the bridge of his nose. He smiled, revealing flawless white teeth. Dana's heart was pounding. She couldn't seem to put any words together. She took a deep breath and managed to smile back. A wide smile that was meant to say everything she couldn't find the words for. *I hope you had a great summer. I think you're the awesomest boy in grade six. I'm so glad you're sitting next to me.*

Unfortunately, Jason didn't seem to get the message. "Ah, I think you might have something stuck in your teeth."

Dana stopped smiling. She unhooked her lip from where it caught and ran her tongue over the bumps of her new braces, feeling for bits of toast crust. As her cheeks started to overheat, Dana looked down and pretended to arrange things in her desk. She heard Jason talking to Trey. And she heard Mickey.

"Dana, Dana, she's got new tracks, but there's no train-a!"

Aargh. Mickey.

Four

IF CLASS WAS weird, cross-country practice was even weirder. Their running coach, Miss Marchand, always got right down to business and called a practice after school on the first day. Dana and Janelle had run together since joining the team in grade three. In races, Nelly was always the first Emery runner in, with Dana never far behind. It felt strange to be warming up behind the school without her friend.

Amber and Gina ran up and tossed their water bottles on the grass. Amber adjusted her headband and Gina checked her phone before they started doing stretches. They had both been on the team last year. They were nice enough girls, but Dana didn't really consider them close friends. Amber was super-serious and never smiled. All she talked about was running, and it made Dana tired just listening to her. Gina seemed cool, but she always left right after practice.

Neta Pederson quietly slipped into the circle. She'd moved to Emery halfway through grade five, and Dana didn't know her well yet. Neta was the kind of girl who blended in easily, so easily she almost disappeared. She wasn't tall or short. She wasn't fat or thin. Her hair was medium length, medium color. She was ordinary in every way. She was also very, very shy.

"Hi." Neta looked around the circle. "I thought I'd come and try out this year. Running. You know. On the team."

Amber looked mildly irritated. She looked around the group. "What do you think our chances are without Janelle?"

"If we have to run without Janelle, maybe we should try running for Janelle," said Neta, smiling brightly. Amber ignored her and started running down the trail. Gina followed. Neta's smile faded.

"Don't worry," said Dana. "Amber's just a little intense. You'll get used to it. Finish the warm-up with me and then we'll go talk to Coach." Miss Marchand currently had her hands full with a bunch of eager grade threes whose warm-up looked more like a tackle football game.

Dana stretched her fingers down to her toes. That's when she saw them. Janelle's shoes. White with blue stripes. Neta was wearing the same shoes Janelle always wore. Janelle called them her lucky running shoes and refused to wear any other kind. Dana's eyes blurred, and she shook her head to clear them.

"You okay?" Neta asked.

Dana nodded. "I'm fine. Come on."

Practice was tough, but Dana felt good. She'd been running all summer. She hadn't had much else to do with Janelle away. Right after the accident, Dana's mom hadn't let her ride her bike anywhere. She was scared Dana might get in an accident too. So Dana had started running wherever she had to go. Things eased up after a few weeks, and her mother said Dana could take her bike out again, but only if she went with her brother, Dale.

When she'd asked Dale to ride with her, he'd thrown her a look that could have melted her bicycle into a puddle. So Dana had done a lot of running.

When practice was over, Dana went to unlock her bike. Inside her helmet she found a note from Dale, saying he'd already left with his friends. They were supposed to ride home together. She shrugged and put on her helmet, then said goodbye to the others.

"Bye, Dana. Say hi to Janelle for me," said Neta.

Dana stiffened. She *should* go see Janelle now. But she was way too hot and sweaty. Then again, Nelly knew all about being gross and sweaty after practice. She wouldn't care. Before she could change her mind again, Dana starting pedaling in the direction of Janelle's house. It bugged her that Julia had been to see her so much. She leaned her bike against the big tree in front of Janelle's house as she always did and knocked on the door. Mrs. Murphy answered.

"Dana, it's wonderful to see you! How have you been?"

"Fine, thanks, Mrs. Murphy. I was wondering if I could see Janelle."

"I'm afraid she's asleep, dear. Julia was here earlier, filling her in on news from the first day at school. Now she's having a little nap before dinner. She's still so tired all the time." Mrs. Murphy smiled sadly. "But I'll tell her you were here."

"Oh. All right," said Dana. "Would tomorrow be okay to stop by? Right after school?" she asked. She had to get there before Julia could.

"Tomorrow she has to go back to the hospital for some X-rays. If things look good, we're hoping she can leave the wheelchair behind."

"Okay, how about Thursday?"

"I'm afraid she has to go to physio. Can you come by Friday?"

"I've got a cross-country meet. Our first one of the season."

"Oh, I'll miss those." Mrs. Murphy sighed and leaned against the doorframe. She had always come to the races and cheered the girls on. They could hear her voice all the way across the course. This had always made Nelly cringe, but Dana thought it was great.

Mrs. Murphy put a hand on Dana's shoulder. "Do your best, Dana. Okay? I'll be thinking about you. Go Eagles!" She smiled. "Listen, Janelle's grandparents are coming for the weekend, so it will be busy here, but if everything goes according to plan, Janelle's hoping to be at school Monday."

"Monday?"

"We'll try. I'll tell her you were here."

"Thanks, Mrs. Murphy."

Five

ON MONDAY MORNING Dana was so excited she had barely been able to eat breakfast. Janelle would be at school, and she couldn't wait to see her. And she couldn't wait to tell her about last Friday's cross-country race. She started pedaling faster. Dale and Dana had started out on their bikes together that morning, but by the time they turned the first corner, Dale was already way ahead. Dana didn't mind. She didn't like being told to hurry up all the time, and she could understand that he didn't want to show up with his little sister in tow. She also secretly hoped that one morning she would run into Jason Elwood. She knew he biked in too. She had checked twice this morning to make sure nothing was stuck in her teeth and had purposely not put the elastic band around her ankle so she wouldn't look ridiculous if he turned up. They hadn't exactly gotten off to a great start, but things could only get better from here.

Dana cruised along, thinking about how good it would be to see Janelle and catch up on everything. She was nearly at school when her bike pedals locked unexpectedly. She almost fell, throwing her left foot out to steady herself. But her right foot wouldn't move. Her jeans had gotten caught in the chain. She couldn't believe it. She pulled on the jeans. She fiddled with the chain. She couldn't get unstuck! She looked around. Dale was long gone. She tried the chain again, but it wouldn't budge. She yanked on the jeans. No luck. She didn't want to tear them. They were brand new. Aargh. How was she going to get to class with a bicycle attached to her leg?

Dana shuffled over to the curb, dragging the bike with her. She sat. And waited. Would she really have to wait until school was over for Dale to come by? No, worse. When she didn't show up, the school would call her mother. She would panic, thinking Dana had had some kind of accident. Once she found out where Dana was and realized she was fine, she'd be angry with Dana for not riding in with her brother. Then Dale would be in trouble, and he would be mad at her too. It was a no-win situation.

Dana picked up a few small pebbles and tossed them half-heartedly into a puddle beside the curb. They made sad little plopping sounds and sent tiny ripples along the surface of the water. When she heard the first bell go at the school, she flopped backward onto the grass. Dana wondered how long it would take for someone to find her. She had just started looking for shapes in the clouds when she heard a noise. Awkwardly, she sat up and shifted so she could look behind her. At first she didn't see anything, but then she heard the noise again. A little dog was peering at her from under a bush not far away. His long black-and-brown hair hung over his eyes.

"Hey there," said Dana. "Are you going to keep me company? I seem to be stuck here."

Dana waited. The dog didn't move.

"No? I could really use a friend."

A bike suddenly skidded up next to her. "Need help?"

Jason! His timing was perfect, although this wasn't exactly the kind of meeting she'd been hoping for. Dana's cheeks burned with embarrassment, but she was also relieved.

"Yeah, I guess. Thanks." She hopped up, trying to haul her bike up with her.

"Here, let me." Jason reached for her hand to steady her. Then he pulled her bike up straight. While he went to work on the chain, Dana pressed her hand against her heart to try to slow it down. The hand that Jason had held. It tingled.

After a minute, Jason stood up again. "Whew. You were good and stuck."

"Well, my mom always says, *if you're going to do something—*"

"*Do it right*? Yeah, my mom says that too." They laughed. He had a great laugh, Dana thought.

Jason wiped his hands on the back of his jeans and began feeling around in his jacket pocket. "Hey, I've got something for you."

"You do?" Dana's eyes lit up.

"It's something pretty special," said Jason. "I found it the other day, and now I know it's meant just for you."

"Really?" *He had something for her? He thought she was special?* She held out her hand. It trembled a little.

Jason dropped an elastic band into her outstretched palm.

"Ta-da! So you won't get caught again," he said. "It's a really strong one. Is it perfect or what?"

"Yeah," said Dana. "Thanks."

Jason was already up on his own bike. "Better hurry."

Dana watched him as he biked away. She got on her bike and looked over at the little dog still hiding under the bush. "Isn't he the greatest?"

The dog gave a quick bark in reply. Dana laughed. "Well, I've gotta go. See you later, Buddy."

Dana got inside just as the last bell rang. Mickey looked at her chewed-up jeans and the grease on her hands and started singing, "Dana, Dana, got caught up in her chain-a." Dana ignored him. As she made her way to the sink at the back of the classroom to wash her hands, she saw Janelle. Janelle! She'd almost forgotten. Her friend was back! Everyone was crowded around talking to her. She had the same beautiful, long blond hair. Same bright smile. Same tinkly laugh. Same white-and-blue shoes. Or shoe. Her left leg was still in a cast and stuck out straight in front of her. There was a pair of crutches stowed underneath the desk too. And the desk was at the very back of the room. Next to Julia's.

Dana felt a sting of guilt for not saving Janelle a seat and making her sit next to Julia. Maybe Dana could ask to move her desk to the back. But that meant she wouldn't be sitting next to Jason anymore. Dana shook her head. She wanted to give her friend a big hug and tell her how good it was to see her. She just needed to wash her hands first. As Dana turned off the faucet, she heard Mr. Bartholomew clear his throat. "All right, everyone, find your seats, please. We're ready to begin."

The crowd around Janelle thinned. Dana wanted to talk to her, but now wasn't the best time. She threw her friend a quick smile, but Janelle was busy looking for something inside her desk. Instead, Dana locked eyes with Julia, who smiled sweetly and rested her hand on the back of Janelle's chair.

"Welcome back, everyone. We have a familiar face in class again today. Janelle, it's good to have you back with us. We were very sorry to hear about the accident."

"Yes," came a voice from the back of the room. But it wasn't Janelle's. It was Julia's. "It's been so hard on her and her entire family." Everyone turned to look at Julia. "It was touch and go at first. She spent her whole summer in the hospital, far from home." She paused, and everyone thought she might cry, but then she drew in a deep, raggedy breath and finished. "But here she is, looking better than ever. It's great to have my best friend back."

Dana stared straight ahead. She felt the words fly through the air like arrows and stick solidly into her shoulders.

Six

ONLY A HALF hour of class had gone by. Time was going so slowly. Dana looked back longingly. *She* should be the one sitting beside Janelle. Julia had moved her desk right up against Janelle's. They were sharing a math textbook, and Julia was explaining something. Dana could have done that. She looked over at Jason, but he was talking to Mickey.

When the bell finally rang for recess, Dana jumped up and headed for the back of the classroom. Julia had gone to her locker, so Dana slid into her desk.

"Hi, Janelle."

"Dana. How are you?"

Dana shook her head. "How are *you*?" she asked.

"I'm okay. Getting there."

"I was at your house."

"I know. My mom told me."

Julia came back and stood beside her desk.

"Excuse me." She tapped Dana's shoulder. When Dana got up, Julia slid back into the seat and placed Janelle's lunch bag on top of her desk. "Anything else you need, Janelle?"

"Yes, anything I can do?" asked Dana quickly.

"No, that's it, I think. Thanks, Julia."

"No problem. That's what best friends are for."

Julia smiled and took out her own snack. "I told Mr. B. I would stay in with you during recess, and he said that was a good idea. I can help you with the stuff you missed."

"Oh. Okay. I have missed a lot." Janelle looked up at Dana. "So, my mom said you had your first run already."

"Yes. Oh, Nelly, it was so awesome. We—" Avery and Allie Grant came over and asked Janelle if they could sign her cast.

"Sure," said Janelle. "Let me just see if I can find something to write with." She began to poke around in her desk.

"Here you go," said Julia, producing a twelve-pack of permanent markers in a rainbow of colors. "I bought these especially for cast signing."

Janelle grinned. "Awesome." She held them out for the twins to pick a color. "Thanks, Julia."

"Dana," said Julia. She motioned to Dana to come closer and lowered her voice. "I can't believe you are talking to Janelle about cross-country. She obviously can't run this season. That is so insensitive."

"But she asked me…"

"Of course she did. She's such a sweetie. But I don't think you need to rub it in."

"I'm not rubbing it in. I just wanted to tell her how great the team did on Friday. I got third. I've never gotten third in my life. I got a ribbon!" Dana opened her fist to show Julia the green ribbon rolled carefully inside. "I want to give it to Janelle," she continued. "Neta said if we couldn't run with Janelle, we could at least run for Janelle, and so…"

Julia smiled tightly. "Just remember, Dana, that talking about things Janelle can't do will not make her feel better. We want to make her feel better, don't we?"

Dana nodded. "Well, of course…"

"Besides," continued Julia, "if I remember correctly, when Janelle ran she was always in front of you, wasn't she? So third place isn't really worth mentioning. You probably only placed because Janelle wasn't in the race. She would have earned that ribbon on her own, don't you think?"

Dana was quiet. Maybe that was true. She remembered standing beside Neta just before the race started. Neta had smiled and held her hand up for a high five. "For Janelle?"

Dana had high-fived her. "For Janelle." She had run the whole race with this in mind—that she was running for her friend. But maybe Julia was right. Maybe it had been a stupid idea. She quickly stuffed the ribbon into the front pocket of her jeans.

Janelle inspected the colorful additions to her cast as Avery and Allie skipped away. Then she turned back to Dana. "Sorry about that. What were you going to say?"

"Mmm…nothing. I forget."

Janelle raised an eyebrow. Dana looked away.

"Do you want to sign my cast?"

"Sure."

When Dana asked Mr. B. if she could stay inside to help Janelle too, he said one friend was enough.

Seven

THE LAST HALF of September was wet. It rained almost every single day. Dana's dad was busy cleaning up gardens and raking leaves. "I see the rain's not hurting you any, Dana," he said one night at supper. "You're growing like a weed!"

Dana was still biking to school. When she complained that her lunch was soggy, her mother began packing all her food in snap-lid containers. When she complained that her schoolwork was getting wet inside her backpack, her mother found special waterproof folders that would *do the trick*. When she complained that water had actually dripped out of her clarinet in band class, her mother dug out an extra-large, bright-blue rain poncho from the basement. Dana felt like a giant bird noisily flapping its massive wings in the wind. Every morning she'd look at the raindrops on the kitchen window and groan. Her mother would smile and run a hand over Dana's hair. "You're not made of sugar, you know. You won't melt."

At school, Dana would hang the poncho on the door of her half-open locker, and it would drip water all over the floor. Mr. Parker, the janitor, started leaving a mop and bucket for her so she could wipe up the puddle. She would shake the water out of her crazy, curly hair and Mickey would sing, "Dana, Dana, has come in from the rain-a."

After school, her cross-country team would run. It was muddy, but they were doing well in the Friday races. Amber, who knew most of the runners on all of the teams and how they usually placed, thought they might even have a shot at the city championship. It was less than three weeks away, and Miss Marchand was so excited that she had them running every day. It didn't take any persuading. The girls were excited too.

When Mrs. Murphy came to pick up Janelle in the afternoons, she would wave to the girls and cheer them on as they ran. Then Janelle would come out on her crutches. She would watch, but she didn't seem all that interested. Instead, she'd be talking to Julia, who was usually carrying Janelle's backpack and a big umbrella.

Dana had tried to talk to Nelly a few times at lunch, but she didn't know what to talk about. Julia was always sending her looks that told her she was saying the wrong things. Gradually, she stopped talking at all and just sat quietly while the other girls chatted. Julia had lots to say anyway, and Janelle didn't seem to notice. A couple of times a week, Dana noticed that Janelle and Julia weren't even around at lunch. Amber said they were working on something together in the library. Still catching up on homework maybe? Why hadn't Janelle asked Dana for help? When Miss Marchand asked for someone to work with the runners in grades three and four at lunch every other day, Dana saw no reason not to volunteer.

Today, though, Dana knew exactly what to talk to Janelle about. She decided to walk over to Janelle's house right after supper so she could talk to her without Julia being around to give her one of her looks. Mr. B. had assigned a big geography project about biomes. Dana and Janelle had always worked together on things like this. During their last week in grade five, their teacher had told them about some of the things they could look forward to doing in grade six. She'd mentioned the biomes project. Janelle and Dana had looked at each other and given each other a nod and a thumbs-up. They made the best partners.

Dana had already done a bit of research and written down a few ideas. She'd taken an umbrella along in case it started raining again. When Janelle asked which topic Dana had in mind, she would hand her the umbrella as a hint. The tropical rainforest. Janelle would love it. Working on this assignment together was just what they needed to make things normal again.

She ran up the steps to Janelle's house, leaned her umbrella against the wall and rang the bell. The door swung open. Julia.

"Hi, Dana."

Dana took a step backward. "Is…is Janelle here?"

"Of course. We're working on our project," she said.

"You mean the geography project?" Dana asked.

"We're doing the tropical rainforest. What about you? Who's your partner?"

"I, umm…" said Dana, recovering slowly. "I'm going to do it by myself. I work better by myself anyway."

Janelle appeared in the hallway. "Dana! Come in. Do you need something?"

"No." Dana shook her head. "I was just running by and thought I'd stop and say hi. So, umm, hi."

"Hi," said Janelle. She shifted uncomfortably. "Did you—"

"Well," Dana interrupted, "I'd better keep running. Got to get lots of practice. Bye!" She turned quickly and ran back down the steps.

"Dana, wait!" Janelle called from the door.

Dana skidded to a halt, sucked in her breath and turned back hopefully. "Yes?"

"You forgot your umbrella."

✧

A week later, Dana tucked the shoebox containing her diorama of the tundra under her poncho and headed for school. She'd meant to ask Dale to help her carry everything, but he was already gone. She should have walked and kept everything nice and dry under her umbrella, as her mother had suggested, but it was too late for that now. The poncho would have to do.

Dana was a little unsteady, riding one-handed. She just needed to take it slowly and carefully. When she was halfway down the driveway, the front of the poncho suddenly flew up in the wind, completely blinding her. She careened down the drive and, before she could stop herself, crashed headlong into a row of recycling bins. She flew off her bike, landing on a stack of soggy newspapers. The shoebox shot out of her hand and went skidding down the sidewalk.

Dana jumped to her feet, yanked off the poncho, balled it up and threw it into one of the boxes. Breathing heavily, she surveyed the mess. Everyone else put one blue box out. The Davis family always had three or four. Her mom was a recycling fanatic and didn't let a single piece end up in the trash. Grumbling, Dana righted the boxes and gathered up all the cans and bottles that had spilled out over the sidewalk and onto the road. She chased after the cardboard pieces that had escaped and were cartwheeling in the wind.

With her shoebox once again stuffed under one arm, Dana got back on her bike. She could feel water spraying up behind her the whole ride in. She squished into class just ahead of the bell and plunked her dripping diorama on the shelf. The iceberg she'd made so carefully out of sugar cubes was melting. The gelatin river was running. Everything she'd made was completely biodegradable, and that's what it was doing now. She pulled down a sheet of paper towel and tried to dry things a little.

Mickey came in, took one look and started to laugh. "Dana, Dana," he sang, "has a skunk stripe stain-a."

Dana was angry. She wheeled around. "Mickey!"

Just then Jason appeared. His timing was perfect again. He really was her knight in shining armor.

"Maybe you'd better give it a rest with the jingles, Mick," he said. He glanced over at the shoebox and winced. "Global warming?"

Dana sighed and then smiled. "It's a big problem."

"So I see. Still biking in?" he asked.

She nodded.

"Cool. I just wanted to tell you…"

Dana held her breath. *What did he want to tell her? That he didn't care if she was a muddy mess? That he thought she was the cutest girl in grade six anyway?*

"You forgot to take the elastic band off your ankle."

Dana let her breath out again like a leaky balloon. "Oh," she said. "Thanks." She reached down and slipped off the elastic band. She looked at the puddle that had formed at her feet. She looked at her soggy shoebox. She looked at Jason walking away with Mickey and then at Janelle chatting with Julia, all the while playing with the elastic band in her hand. Suddenly, it snapped. *Ouch!* It was supposed to have been a really strong one. But she guessed things could only stretch so far before they broke. Water dripped out of Dana's hair. Her eyes stung as she busied herself with her diorama.

"Okay, everyone," called Mr. B. "Time to find your seats. Dana, are you okay back there? Do you need any help?"

Dana shook her head. She cleared her throat and wiped her face. It had just been a really bad morning. That's all. Things couldn't possibly get any worse. She took a deep breath and tried to smile. Like her mother always said, if crying wasn't going to do any good, she might as well laugh. Besides, there was no time for tears. Dana had noticed something when she'd confronted Mickey. She was taller than he was. That meant she was almost taller than Jason. She'd have to do something. Fast.

It rained all day. When Dana ran up the steps and into the house that afternoon, she almost crashed into her mother taking off her boots just inside the door. Dana was surprised to see the blue poncho hanging on one of the hooks in the hallway.

"Oh, Dana, you're home. I just got in too. It's a soaker, isn't it? Why in the world aren't you wearing your poncho? I found it in the recycling."

Dana described her encounter with the blue boxes. She didn't say anything about how the rest of the morning had gone.

"Oh no." Her mom laughed and gave her a hug. "Are you hurt?"

Dana paused, then shook her head.

"Why don't you go and get dried off. I'll make some tea." Her mother disappeared into the kitchen.

Dana looked over at the poncho hanging on the hook and wrinkled her nose. Maybe her problems were not going to go away as easily as she thought.

Eight

IT WAS OFFICIAL. The cross-country team had had its wettest but most successful season in the school's history. In last Friday's city championship, Dana had placed third in the race for grade-six girls. Neta was seventh.

"Dana, that was amazing!" gushed a soggy Miss Marchand when all the girls had crossed the finish line. "And Neta, you came out of nowhere. I didn't even know you could run like that! Amber, Gina, well done!"

Mrs. Murphy had planned to come out to the race with Janelle, but it was too wet. She'd left a message saying she was sorry, but she was afraid Janelle might slip with her crutches and hurt herself again. *Go Eagles!* she had shouted into the phone.

The team had come in fourth place overall! Each member received a beautiful, gleaming yellow ribbon. Even Amber had to smile. Miss Marchand had told the girls she was going to wear her coach's jersey to school Monday morning and encouraged them to wear their ribbons. *Let's celebrate!* she'd said. Remembering what had happened last time, Dana left her ribbon at home. Biking in, however, she did share her big news with the little dog. Almost every day since she'd first seen him, Dana had stopped to look for him, and often she found him hiding under the same bush. "Hey, Buddy," she called out to him this morning. "We did it! We won fourth at the cross-country championship." He wagged his tail in response.

At lunch, Beverley Tran met Dana at her locker and asked to interview her about the race. Beverley was an eighth-grader and in charge of the school newspaper. She had the most beautiful shiny black hair, which swung over her shoulder as she pulled out her notebook. Dana tried to flatten her own wild hair while Beverley uncapped her pen. "So Diana," said Beverley, "tell me about the season and your recent success."

"Well," Dana began, "it's Dana, actually, and—"

"Cross-country, right?"

"Yes."

"You were on the grade-six team?"

"Yes, and—"

"Girls, right?"

"Well, yeah—"

"Just checking the facts. A fourth-place finish, I understand."

"Yes, it's the best the school's ever—"

"And what about you? You finished…?"

"Well, I—"

Julia picked that very moment to jump in. Dana hadn't even known she'd come up beside her. "Beverley," she said, "that kind of article is so cliché. Humdrum. Who cares? They ran, they got sweaty, end of story. Make an announcement, of course, put a picture in the paper, but if you want a real human-interest piece, why don't you come and talk to Janelle Murphy about her accident and brave recovery? It's inspirational. Don't you think so, Dana?"

"Sure I do, but—"

Julia pulled Beverley into the classroom and over to Janelle's desk. Beverley eyed the cast and cocked her head. "What happened?"

"An accident," answered Julia. "She was in the hospital for weeks. It was a life-and-death situation."

Beverley tapped her notebook. She looked from Janelle to Dana and back again. "Okay. What do you say? Will you do an interview with me?"

Janelle looked unsure. "Well, I don't know. I wouldn't know what to say."

Julia jumped in again. "I'll help," she said.

The bell rang. "I'll be back tomorrow at lunch," Beverley said to Janelle and Julia. "Oh, and Diana," she called over her shoulder on her way out, "get your team together then too. We'll get a picture."

Nine

MID-OCTOBER, AND it hadn't rained for an entire week. Everything seemed better when the sun was shining. Dana stuck her tongue out at the blue poncho hanging on its hook in the hallway and went to get her bike out of the garage. The sun was warm on her shoulders. The leaves on the trees flashed red, yellow and orange.

Dana tried to hang on to her happy feeling, but she found herself pedaling more and more slowly. It was becoming harder and harder for her to go to school. Janelle and Julia were always together now, and Dana noticed that more of the girls were going to the library at lunch. She didn't know what they were doing, and she was afraid of Julia's reaction if she asked.

Dana kept an eye out for Jason, especially when she reached the spot where he'd helped her with her bike chain. But there was no Jason in sight. At least she still had one friend she could count on. She coasted along the curb and looked for the little dog. Maybe she could coax him out this time. She didn't see him at first. Then, without warning, he shot out from under the bush, barking furiously.

"Whoa, Buddy, what's up?"

He growled and showed his sharp little teeth.

"Okay, okay." Dana thought he might bite and immediately took off again on her bike. When she looked back, the dog had disappeared from the sidewalk. What had she done to deserve that?

When she got to the school, she saw Jason's bike was already in the rack. The boys were out playing in the field. Janelle's parents' car pulled up to the sidewalk. Before Dana could even take a step toward it, Julia ran up from the opposite direction and opened the door. She grabbed Janelle's backpack, and the two of them walked into the school. Dana rolled her eyes. Janelle had gotten her cast off last week. Couldn't she open the car door herself now and carry her own stuff? Dana bit her lip. *That was mean.* She busied herself with her bike lock until the bell rang and she could go inside.

Mr. Bartholomew assigned a whole page of math problems first thing. Dana had a hard time concentrating. Then he gave them half an hour for silent reading. Dana spent most of it staring at the same three words. "Okay, class," Mr. B. said at last, rubbing his hands together excitedly. "What do you say we shift gears now? Today we start a unit on poetry."

His announcement was met with groans. Mr. B. laughed. "Come on now. Give it a chance. You just might like it! We'll read some poems by different authors over the next few days, but I want to begin by having you write your own poem. Poetry is a great way to express your feelings. Don't search too hard for a topic, and don't worry too much about technique. Just write about what's on your mind. Write from the heart. I'll give you five minutes."

Dana tried to clear her head. She took a deep breath and rolled her shoulders to loosen them up. She tried to think of poetry-like things—waves, clouds, sunshine—but nothing came to her. *Write what's on your mind*, Mr. B. had said. She did have a lot on her mind. Anger and confusion churned around inside her like an overloaded washing machine. She felt like she might burst. She was too hurt to write about Janelle, too angry to write about Julia and too embarrassed to write about Jason. But she had to write something. The minutes ticked away. She started to breathe more quickly, and her hands got sweaty.

"Two more minutes," said Mr. B.

Don't search too hard for a topic, he had said. Suddenly Dana had an idea. She wrote quickly, but her pen could barely keep up to her thoughts. She had just finished when Mr. B. said time was up, and she didn't have a chance to read it over.

"Okay, everyone," said Mr. B. "It's almost recess. We have just enough time to have three of you read your poems to the class. Let's have Tyler, Charlotte and…Dana, how about you?"

Read it? In front of everyone?

Tyler's finished product was a four-line poem about baseball that made everyone, especially Trey and Greg, cheer loudly. Charlotte had written a lovely free-verse poem about a sunny day at the lake. The whole class clapped when she finished reading it.

"Very nice," said Mr. B. "Dana? Your turn."

Dana looked down at her page and then up at her teacher.

"Is it from the heart?" he asked.

She nodded.

"Then let us have it," encouraged Mr. B.

Dana stood up. She took a deep breath. "Dogs," she began. She looked around at her classmates. They were all watching her, waiting to hear what she had to say. She cleared her throat and began again.

DOGS

Dogs, dogs, dogs, dogs,
they hide under bushes, they hide behind logs.

Their teeth are sharp, they're full of drool,
they chase you on your way to school.
They're small and quiet and have long hair,
they listen and you think they care.
They look so cute with their round little eyes,
they look like pals, but it's all lies.
We were friends, or so I thought.
Shows the kind of friend I've got.

There was total silence for a few seconds as everyone puzzled over the poem. Dana glanced over at Janelle, who had a strange look on her face. Then the bell rang for recess, and the students bolted.

"Kickball!" yelled Trey. "Jay, bring the ball!"

"Well," said Mr. B. He looked at Dana, still standing beside her desk with her paper in her hand. "That was different, Dana. Lots of, umm, emotion. Is everything okay?"

"I think so." *I hope so.*

Dana quickly made her way to the back of the room where the girls had gathered, pulling on jackets and snacking on celery, crackers and chocolate-chip cookies. If she could just get Janelle alone for one minute, she could explain everything. She could still fix this.

"Our dog would never bite anyone," Avery was saying.

"No way," added Allie, shaking her head.

"My grandma has the cutest little dog," said Gina. "I just melt when he looks at me with those little puppy eyes."

"Does Dana even have a dog?" asked Julia.

"I don't think so," answered Janelle.

She didn't think so? Janelle knew Dana didn't have any pets. Did she think Dana wouldn't have told her if they'd gotten a dog? And why were they talking about her as if she wasn't even there?

Before Dana could tell them about Buddy and explain what had happened earlier that morning, the girls had already started talking about something else. And there was no way Dana was going to be able to talk to Janelle by herself without it being awkward.

Dana slipped down the hall toward the bathrooms. *Dana, Dana, would things ever be normal again-a?* She saw a group of girls from grades seven and eight pointing at something on the bulletin board and stopped to see what was so exciting. She peered over heads and shoulders, and when she read the posting her heart leaped. This was her ticket back to the way things were supposed to be. She knew it.

"I put my name on the list," said Dana, bounding back into the classroom. She was so excited, she couldn't stand still. "Is anyone else going to? Did you, Amber? McKayla? Nelly, come on—the list is up. Put your name on it!"

"What list?" Janelle asked. "What are you talking about?"

"The volleyball sign-up list. We talked about this all through grade five, how we could finally play on the volleyball team this year, and now the list is up! It's in the hallway. There are tryouts next week. Come on!"

Janelle's smile faded. "Dana, I can't…"

"What do you mean? You love volleyball. Your cast is off. We've—" Dana stopped. The cast had only been off for four days. She sucked in her breath. "You don't think that by next week…"

She faltered. "No, I'm sorry, Nelly. I just got too excited. I didn't think it through. Never mind. It doesn't matter. I'll take my name off."

Janelle shook her head. "Don't be silly," she said softly. "You can still play."

"But we were going to do it together."

"I know." Janelle sighed. "But you can still play. You should play."

Dana watched as Janelle turned to put her lunch bag away. She walked slowly and still had a definite limp. *Why had she brought up volleyball in the first place? What was wrong with her?* "Janelle…" she called after her.

Julia moved in beside her. "You know, Dana, I don't think a real friend would have put her name on that list in the first place."

"But we were planning to sign up since last year. You don't understand."

"I don't think you understand. Things have changed, Dana. Can't you see that? Can't you see how sad you've made her?"

Can't you see how sad this makes me? "Nelly said—"

"That's another thing I've been meaning to talk to you about. Why do you keep calling her Nelly? Her name is Janelle."

Dana felt a hard lump form in her throat. "FYI, Julia, I've been calling her Nelly since we were in kindergarten."

Julia crossed her arms. "FYI, Dana, we're not in kindergarten anymore. Besides, Janelle's been through a life-threatening, life-changing experience. I don't think we should be calling her baby names anymore."

"Well," Dana said, trying to keep her voice even as she watched Janelle make her way back toward them, "why don't we let Janelle decide?"

"Okay. Why don't we?" Julia smiled broadly. "Janelle, Dana and I were just talking about those silly names people used to call us when we were in, like, kindergarten? Remember?"

Janelle smiled. She seemed glad for the shift in conversation. "Ugh," she said. "Don't remind me. So embarrassing."

"Don't you think it's time they disappeared for good?"

"Oh," said Janelle, "I thought they *had* disappeared." She shivered. "I just hated that!" She rolled her eyes.

Julia looked at Dana. She didn't say a word, but the look on her face said, *I told you so*.

"Hey," said Janelle, "it's my turn to feed the fish. Anyone want to help me?

Julia smiled. "Sure."

Dana didn't move. Janelle had been through a life-changing experience. Apparently, that meant friend-changing too. Dana didn't go over to the fish tank. She didn't go back out to the hallway either. She decided she was going to keep her name on the list for tryouts next week. Practices would give her something new to do at recess.

Dana scanned the list again just before she left the school that afternoon to make sure her name was still there. It was. Hers was the only grade-six name on it.

Ten

ON THE DAY of the tryouts, Dana left the classroom without a word to the other girls. She changed into a T-shirt and shorts and made her way over to the gym. She pulled open the door and peeked inside. There were a dozen or so girls already serving and bumping balls all over the gym and another half dozen tying their shoes, stretching or pulling their hair up into ponytails. Dana sighed. There were plenty of girls here to form a team. They didn't really need anyone from grade six. She considered leaving, but the shouts and the sound of the volleyballs hitting the floor made her hesitate. She liked volleyball. A lot.

Dana spotted the coach, Mr. Finch, pulling volleyballs out of an enormous mesh bag. "Dana!" he said as he stood up. "Here to try out?"

She nodded.

"Where's everyone else from your class?"

She shrugged.

"That's okay. We're glad you came. We're just about to get started." He blew two sharp blasts on his whistle, and all the girls stopped what they were doing and crowded around, balls tucked under one arm. "Okay, ladies," he called. "I want to welcome you all to volleyball tryouts. Now, they're called tryouts for a reason—I really want to see everyone trying. Let's give it our best. All right?"

The girls nodded and cheered.

"Great. Let's start with some serving. Half of you make a line on this side of the net, and half of you go to the other side. One player from this group will serve the ball over, then one from the other group will catch it and serve it back, okay?"

Dana joined the end of the line on the far side of the gym. That way she could watch for a few minutes before serving. Some of the girls served low, so the ball hit the net and bounced back. They had to run up and catch the ball themselves and roll it over to the other side. Some served high and hit the rafters. Some served sideways and hit the bleachers. But a few were able to serve the ball perfectly. The ball would soar over the net and hit so hard that Dana thought it might make a hole in the floor. "Crater maker!" the girls would yell. Dana's first serve hit the net, and she felt the heat in her face as she ran to catch the ball. Her second serve went over, but it was soft and would have been easy to return if they'd actually been playing another team. Her third attempt wasn't bad, but no one yelled *crater maker* either. What was she doing here?

The whistle blew again. "All right, girls," said Mr. Finch. "Good job. Now I want you to organize yourselves into groups of three. Make sure someone in your group has a ball. One of you will bump it, one of you will set it, and one of you will tip it over the net. Then switch positions. Got it?"

The girls scattered to form groups with their friends, and Dana was left standing awkwardly beside the coach. Two girls jogged back from the water fountain. "Ah, here we go," said Mr. Finch. "Dana, here are Lisa Torelli and Emily Van Kamp. Why don't you three form a group together?"

Uh-oh. The girls were both in grade eight and had wicked serves. No way would they want her in their group. "Okay," she said.

"Let's go," said Emily.

The girls worked together for a while. Dana was pretty good at bumping and setting but discovered she was really good at jumping and tipping the ball over the net.

"Wow, I wish I could jump like that," said Lisa, coming over to give her a high five.

"Well, I wish I could serve like you do," said Dana, giving Lisa a high five in return.

"I wish you two would get back to the drill so I can show you again how awesome I am," said Emily, and they all laughed.

Mr. Finch outlined a few more drills before blowing his whistle to end the tryouts. "Thank you, ladies," he said. "You've worked hard. You know I'd put you all on the team if I could, but I can only have twelve. The list will be up tomorrow morning. Look for it right away, because our first practice will be at lunch. We're going to have to jump right in. First game is next week!"

Twelve? Yikes. Dana looked around, her dream of playing on the team flickering out. Oh well, she thought. She could always try out again next year.

"See you tomorrow, Dana," called Emily as she ran by.

Tomorrow? A tiny, stubborn flame of hope flared in Dana's heart and dared to start burning again.

Eleven

THE NEXT MORNING, Dana rushed to school in hopes of seeing the list before anyone else got there. She didn't expect to make the team. Still, if her name wasn't there, she'd rather be alone with her disappointment.

The schoolyard was deserted as she wheeled her bike to the racks. Good. She smoothed her hair, took a deep breath and walked inside. As she walked toward the gym, Dana immediately spotted the list taped to the door, but the names were still too small to read. Her heart began to beat more quickly. She walked the last few steps with her eyes closed, then took a deep breath. She opened one eye.

The names blurred together as she scrolled down the list. Dana opened both eyes wide and read it again. Her throat started to hurt. She read it slowly one more time to be sure. Tears welled up in her eyes, and she took off down the hallway. Dana unlocked her bike, threw on her helmet and tore down the street, pedaling like crazy. After several minutes, she began to slow down. Finally, she stopped her bike by the side of the road, propped it up against the curb and sat on the grass. She took in a few deep breaths. Then she smiled. She smiled so wide it almost hurt. She laughed out loud. She'd made it. She'd made the team. She was an Eagle.

After a moment, a bike skidded up beside her. "You're not stuck again, are you?" It was Jason.

"Nope, not today. Look at this stylish Velcro band my mom got me." Dana patted her shin and grinned. Her lip got hung up on her braces, but she didn't even care.

"Nice. What's up? You seem pretty excited about something."

"I made the volleyball team."

"Oh yeah? Congratulations. I knew you would."

"You did?"

"Of course. I've seen you play."

He did?

"And you're tall. That helps."

Hmmm. He'd noticed that too.

"Well, are you coming to school or not? Won't be as much fun without you!" He smiled his bright smile.

Dana's cheeks flamed. *Had he actually just said what she thought he said?* "You bet. I've got a volleyball practice at lunch."

"Yeah?"

"And a game next week!"

"What do you say we get going then? It's pretty cold just sitting out here."

We? Here it was! Her chance to ride in with Jason Elwood. What a great day this was turning out to be. "I know," Dana agreed, hopping onto her bike. "My fingers are freezing. My nose too."

"Yeah, it's red. It looks kind of like a tomato."

A tomato? Couldn't he at least have said a cherry?

Dana had planned to spend most of her time on the bench that first game, but Mr. Finch had other ideas. He had asked Dana to be a blocker because she was tall. This should have made her feel good, but it didn't. She wanted Jason to keep noticing her, but not because she was a giant! Dana scanned the crowd, but she didn't see him even though she'd let it slip more than once during the day that there was going to be a game after school.

The team formed a huddle at their bench. "Eagles on two!" shouted Emily.

"One, two, Eagles!" they all shouted in return. "Let's fly."

Dana laughed. She almost turned to the girl beside her to give her a high five and shout, "For Janelle!" but she caught herself just in time.

Dana was so nervous, she felt like she was shivering all the time. She wasn't the only one. The first serve landed in their end without anyone even moving to touch it. "Eagles," shouted Mr. Finch.

"Wake up! Look alive! You look like statues out there. Let's move!"

When the second serve landed the same way, he called a time-out. "Ladies," he said when the team gathered near the bench. "You've got to loosen up! Come on. Do what I do." He shook his head from side to side. It looked like he had disconnected it from his neck somehow. He jiggled his cheeks. The girls just looked at each other. Was he serious? "Let's go," he said. "We've only got thirty seconds here." He shook his head again. No one else did. Mr. Finch stood up very straight and put his hands on his hips. "Let's go, girls," he said. "Go crazy or go home! I mean it." He shook his head again, and this time all the girls did too. He shook out his legs. The girls copied him. He flapped his arms. The girls did the same. Then he did all three at once.

"Good. Now, again," said Mr. Finch, "with a little more enthusiasm this time."

By the time the thirty seconds were over, the Eagles were back on the court, red-faced but warmed up and ready. The other team was smirking. A few of them were laughing out loud. Not for long though. The next serve was returned with one bump, and the Eagles went on to win the game easily.

Dana had made a couple of good blocks, and the girls had all cheered her on. That had felt really good, like she belonged. Still, when the game was over, the other girls paired off and Dana biked home by herself. Oh well. She plunked her stuff in the hallway and went to take a shower.

Dana looked at herself in the bathroom mirror. She did the head-shaking move Mr. Finch had done, and she laughed. She noticed she had mud splatters on her nose from the bike ride home. As she tried to wipe them off, she saw…oh no. It wasn't mud. She leaned closer. Pimples! Three of them! Crazy, sticky-up hair, chewed-up jeans that were already almost too short and now pimples on her nose! Her tomato nose. *Dana, Dana, is it all in vain-a? What would Jason think now?*

Just when she was beginning to think she'd gotten his attention, she started to wonder if it might be easier just to be like Neta and blend in.

Twelve

EVERYONE WAS OUT of their seats and talking at once. Mr. Bartholomew was standing near the door with his arms folded across his chest and a big grin on his face. Coming into class this morning, the students had found a huge movie poster of *The Wizard of Oz* plastered to the blackboard at the front of the room. Mr. B. had just announced that *Oz* was going to be the school play this year.

"I'm glad to see you're so excited," said Mr. B. when the buzz began to quiet down a little. "I knew you would be. Over the next couple of days, I want you to think about what role you'd like to play. You can choose to be a character or a member of the backstage crew, but we're going to need everyone to be involved somehow. We'll have auditions in a week or so, and then we'll assign parts. There will be acting, singing, costumes, makeup, set design and, most of all, a whole lot of fun! All right, everyone to their seats now, please."

Jason took his seat and leaned toward Dana. "You should try for the lead."

Dana glanced behind her to see if he was talking to someone else, but there was no one there. "What?" she asked.

"You should try for the lead. In the play."

"You mean the part of the Wicked Witch?" asked Mickey, sitting over in row three.

"No," said Jason, shaking his head. "I mean Dorothy. Seriously, I think you'd be great."

"Me?"

"Yeah."

"Really?"

"Really." He nodded. "You like dogs." He cocked his head, trying to remember what it was she'd said about dogs. "Right? And you're funny. I'd like to be the Scarecrow, I think, or maybe the Tin Man. Yeah, the Tin Man," he said with a grin.

He looked at Mickey. "Who do you want to be? A Munchkin?"

Dana sat down at her desk. She'd been thinking of signing up for the backstage crew. *Should she really try for the lead? Jason thought she could do it. Was this the way to make him keep noticing her? But just what did he mean by* funny?

Thirteen

FOR THE NEXT few days, the play was the only thing anyone talked about. Groups of girls walked around outside with their arms linked, chanting, "Follow the yellow brick road." Or they huddled together at their desks, whispering and cackling like witches. Someone was really good at it. *Probably Julia.*

Dana didn't do any chanting or cackling. She felt like she was hovering on the edge of all the excitement. No one was actively excluding Dana, but things just felt different. Her place had always been with Janelle. Now she felt cut off from her roots, rolling around like a tumbleweed.

Jason's words continued to float around in Dana's head. *Should she try out for the lead?* The whole idea made her feel light-headed. It meant learning a lot of lines. It also meant she'd have to sing! Normally, Dana would have asked Janelle her advice, but they weren't really speaking these days. Julia, on the other hand, had lots to say. She couldn't stop talking about how Janelle just *had* to be Dorothy.

"She has such beautiful, long hair that she could wear in pigtails, just like Dorothy," said Julia.

"But it's blond," said Dana.

"So?"

"Doesn't Dorothy have brown hair?"

"And she has the same bubbly personality."

At least, she used to.

"Plus she's so sweet and always trying to help people."

Is she?

"It's a big commitment, but I know she could do it."

Dana bit her lip. "I've been thinking I might try out for the part." It was like all the air went out of the room. Julia didn't say anything for a moment.

"You want to be Dorothy?"

"I don't know. Maybe."

Julia's eyes narrowed. "Don't you think that's a little selfish, Dana?"

"Selfish?"

"Don't you think you've taken enough away from Janelle without taking this too? I thought you would try to help Janelle, to support her. That's what friends do, isn't it?"

Dana wasn't sure what friends did anymore. She was also pretty sure Janelle didn't need her help for anything. She had Julia. "So, you don't think I should try out?"

"Janelle would be a perfect Dorothy," said Julia.

"Of course she would," said Dana. Janelle was good at everything. Good at sports. Good at school. Good at having friends. Small. Pretty. And she had perfect hair. It was annoying how perfect she was.

꒰꒱

Dana went to volleyball practice every other day at recess. The days she didn't have to, she found a nice little sheltered corner beside the gym where no one ever seemed to go. So what if a bunch of the girls had permission to work in the library at recess? Dana had decided it would be fine just to be by herself. She had something else to focus on, something very important. She didn't know what to do about Janelle or Julia or Dorothy, for that matter, but she did know one thing. She liked Jason Elwood, and she was going to tell him. But how? When? Where? Definitely somewhere private and preferably somewhere they could sit down so that she wasn't towering over him. She was growing taller every day. Now was the time.

Dana thought long and hard. Finally, she decided she would send Jason a note. She considered very carefully what it should say and what it should look like. Dear Jason? No way. Love, Dana? Absolutely not. Printing? Handwriting? Hearts and flowers? Too embarrassing. In the end she just stuck a green sticky note inside his desk, asking him to meet her around the corner of the gym at recess on Friday. She didn't sign her name. He'd know where the green paper came from. How many people had frog-shaped sticky notes?

Fourteen

DANA HAD PUT the note in Jason's desk on Tuesday. By Wednesday, she was wondering why she'd done it four days ahead of time. She had wanted lots of time to prepare. Now she knew she'd just given herself lots of time to worry instead. At least she had a volleyball game that afternoon to help keep her mind off things.

The Wesley Wildcats were visiting. They were a tough team. During the warm-up, Dana noticed that they had some great servers. They also had some really tall girls who were very good at tipping the ball back over the net. The Eagles were going to have to be ready. But Dana was distracted.

Every time she thought about the note she'd put in Jason's desk, she got a really weird feeling. Her face got hot, but her insides felt like cold jelly. She was glad she'd written the note, and she was excited about talking to him. But nervous too. A little.

She scanned the crowd starting to fill the bleachers. She didn't see Jason. Janelle hadn't come to watch the game either. Dana wasn't sure why she even bothered looking for her. She shook her head. *Never mind. Concentrate.* She narrowed her focus to only the volleyball. *Watch the ball. Watch the ball.*

She began to anticipate where the ball would go, and every time the Wildcats tried to bump it over the net, Dana was there to block it. She jumped. She blocked. She tipped. She called out to the back row when it went over her head. Time after time she was able to return the ball. It was a tight game. Very tight. It was game point again and again. First for the Eagles. Then for the Wildcats. Neither team could get ahead by the two points they needed to win. Dana tried to ignore the score and kept her focus on the ball.

The Wildcats sent a blistering serve their way. The Eagles sent it back. The Wildcats tried to return it, but the ball hit the net and bounced back on their side. Now Emily had the serve, but she put too much into it and it went out of bounds. The Wildcats served the ball back and the same thing happened. "Easy does it, ladies," called Mr. Finch. "Easy does it."

Lisa Torelli was up. She served the ball way over to the left, and all the Eagles held their breath, thinking it was going to go out. Instead, it landed just inside the line to give the Eagles a point. The Wildcats rolled it back to the other side. Everyone took another deep breath.

"Game point, game point," shouted the fans.

Dana felt tingly all over. Lisa served the ball a second time. It was a good, hard hit. "Crater maker!" yelled the crowd, but the Wildcat player in the middle of the back row managed to get a piece of it and bump it back in their direction.

"Short, it's short!" called the girls behind Dana. But it wasn't. It had just enough oomph to hover right above the net. Dana jumped and tipped the ball so lightly that it dropped to the floor right next to the net. The other side of the net. The other team didn't have a chance. Game point. Emery Elementary had won.

Dana was swarmed by a mob of jumping, screaming girls. Emily pulled her out and put her first in line to shake hands with the Wildcats. Back at their own bench, the girls exchanged hugs and high fives. When the team was finished celebrating at last, Mr. Finch asked Dana and Lisa to stay behind a minute. He called Beverley Tran over.

"Beverley," he said, "I know you were taking pictures at the game, and you've probably got lots of great shots already, but could you please take one of these two young ladies? Lisa was our star server today. Dana made some exceptional plays in the front row."

Beverley tossed the girls a ball, and they held on to it together and grinned while Beverley took the picture. "Okay. It should be in this week's school news," she said.

"Good game," said Lisa.

"You too," said Dana. She felt great. If she could do this, she could do anything. *Meeting Jason? Piece of cake. But would he come?*

Fifteen

HE CAME. WALKING out toward the gym on Friday morning at recess, Dana almost couldn't believe it. He was sitting with his back against the gym wall. She could see his untied shoelaces sprawled over the gravel. Her heart began to pound, and her throat felt tight. She tried not to let her courage slip away as she turned the corner. This was it.

"Hey, Jason."

"Oh, hey, Dana."

Her voice had come out all squeaky. She decided she'd better start with some small talk. Calm her nerves and then build up to what she actually wanted to say. Dana cleared her throat. "How's it going?"

"Good." He jumped up and looked around the corner. "Good." Was he nervous too? She wished he'd sit down again so she could sit down too.

"Nice day."

"Yep."

It was working. Her heart rate was slowing down, and her voice sounded almost normal. Jason, on the other hand, seemed to be getting more and more uptight.

"Ummm, how do you think you did on the math quiz?" Dana asked. "Are you any good at geometry?"

"Math quiz? Ah, not bad. Listen, Dana, I was wondering…"

Dana smiled hopefully. *Maybe this was it. Maybe he was going to say what she was working up the nerve to confess.* "Yes?"

"Ah, I was wondering…Well…" He looked around the corner again. "Listen. Hmm, how do I put this?"

Dana's eyes lit up. "What is it?"

"Do you…do you think you could, ah, leave?"

Huh?

"I don't want to be rude or anything, but I'm kind of waiting for someone." He bit his lip and shifted from side to side. "I'm not positive, but I have a pretty good idea who it might be, and she might not show up if I'm talking to someone else. And if I can't meet with her now…well, I'm going to miss the kickball game!"

Dana could see some of the other boys playing way out at the back of the field. Even from where she stood, she could hear Trey shouting.

"You're—you're waiting for someone?"

"Yeah. I think…well, I think maybe she likes me." He leaned against the gym wall and looked out at the field. "I don't really…well…anyway, I don't want to leave before I talk to her, because I've got to be careful. She's been hurt, and I guess I don't want her to be hurt again. You know?" He looked at Dana.

Hurt? Dana felt her face get hot. *Oh yes, she knew. Same old story all over again. She was getting sick and tired of it.* She waited a moment so her voice would come out normally. "Oh," she said. "I'm sorry." She tried to say it lightly, but her smile was tight. She swallowed hard. She cleared her throat. "I, uh, I hope she comes." Dana turned to go.

"Yeah, we'll see, I guess. I hope it's soon, 'cause man, I'm missing the whole game!"

"Where's Jay?" Trey was shouting. "Anyone know where Jason is?"

Dana took a deep breath and walked away. *You don't know what you're missing, Jason Elwood. You don't even notice bright-green, frog-shaped paper when it's on the desk right beside you! Kickball! Ugh.* Dana felt like kicking Jason in the shins. Instead, she yanked open the door and found the closest girls' bathroom. Hot tears had sprung to her eyes, and she knew her face would be red and puffy. If she could just splash some cold water on it before the bell rang, she might get away without anyone noticing. Not that anyone noticed her these days anyway. *Hmmmph.* She pulled open the bathroom door, then stopped short just before going in. Someone was singing. In an absolutely beautiful, clear voice, someone was singing the words to Dorothy's song from *Oz*. "*Somewhere over the rainbow, skies are blue, and the dreams that you dare to dream really do come true."* The singing was lovely, soft and sweet.

All Dana saw were the singer's feet where she stood in front of the mirrors. That was enough. White-and-blue running shoes. Shoes Dana would know anywhere. She didn't know Janelle could sing like that. It struck her suddenly that there was a lot she didn't know about her best friend. Were they even best friends anymore? Was it all Julia's fault, or had Dana sabotaged the friendship on her own? And why did Jason think Janelle was going to be the one meeting him outside this morning? Janelle knew Dana had liked him forever. She wouldn't try to steal him. Or would she? Was Julia in on this? It was all too complicated. She had to get out of there. She didn't know what she'd do if she saw Janelle go outside and talk to Jason. Especially now that she'd heard her sing. Janelle really was perfect for Dorothy. And if Jason didn't like her already, he would once she got the lead role.

Dana backed away and let the bathroom door swing closed. She shook her head and told herself to calm down. She walked slowly down the hallway, taking deep breaths, and stopped to pick up a copy of the school newspaper. Had the volleyball story made it? The front page didn't even mention volleyball. Instead, it featured a huge picture of Janelle and Julia and an article about the bracelet-making group that met during recess. That's what they had been doing in the library. Proceeds from the bracelets were going to buy toys and games for the children's hospital Janelle had stayed at. Dana didn't remember being invited to make any bracelets. Of course, she'd been busy with running and volleyball and writing stupid notes on frog-shaped paper. They probably hadn't wanted her to be in the group anyway.

It wasn't until she turned to the very last page of the paper that Dana found the volleyball article. The picture had turned out okay, but it was pretty small. *Eagles Win*, read the caption. *Game stars Lisa Torelli and Diana Davis.*

It was the last straw. Dana felt her anger build. Just below the picture was an announcement reminding grade-six students about the upcoming tryouts for their play. Dana crunched the page between her fingers. She decided then and there that she would try out for the lead part. After all, what did she have to lose?

Sixteen

SHE SECOND-GUESSED herself immediately. Dana had gotten a DVD of *The Wizard of Oz* from the library and watched half of it that evening. Dorothy's part was huge! All those lines. All that singing and skipping! What was she getting herself into? Brushing her hair before going to bed, Dana tried putting it in pigtails. The DVD Dorothy had lovely, wavy, brown hair in pigtails that bounced on her shoulders. Dana's stuck out from the sides of her head like a set of straw pom-poms. She sighed, dropping the brush back down on her dresser, and turned out the light.

Sleep did not come easily. Thoughts whirled around in her head. She dreamed she was skipping down a yellow brick road and leaves were falling from the trees—hundreds of them, thousands. Only they weren't leaves, they were frog-shaped sticky notes. And they were croaking, "Dana, Dana, is slipping down the lane-a." And it was true. The notes were slippery, and Dana was having a hard time making her way through them. Every so often she'd fall and completely disappear under an enormous pile of them. It was terrible. Then it started to rain, but the raindrops weren't drops at all. They were kickballs and volleyballs sailing in from all sides. Dana began to run. *Over the rainbow. I've got to get over the rainbow to where the skies are blue.* She fought her way up the rainbow hill, but the whole time Munchkins were firing elastic bands at her. *Ow!* Dana woke with a start. She sat up and turned on the lamp on her bedside table. Maybe a glass of milk would help her sleep.

Dana's mother was standing by the kitchen table, sorting and cutting material into pieces that could be used for quilts. Besides making quilts and pillow covers herself, she also gave away bags of pieces to other quilt-making groups. All kinds of people dropped off bags of their old clothes and fabrics at Dana's house. They were stored in what Dana called the recycling room. Every so often, Dana's mother would pull out a bag or two and start separating the contents into items that could still be used and sold in thrift stores, things that could be cut down and used for quilt pieces, and material that could be used for rags.

Dana sat down at the table with her glass of milk. Her mother looked up and smiled.

"Trouble sleeping?" she asked.

"Hmmm."

"Not a bad dream, I hope."

Dana didn't answer. She wouldn't know where to begin.

"Something on your mind?"

Lots of things. Dana shrugged.

"You know, a patient showed me a really interesting article today from a magazine she'd been reading in the waiting room. It was all about how car makers are using all kinds of recycled materials in the new vehicles they're putting out.

Recycled cotton for dashboards and insulation. Recycled water bottles in seats and armrests. What do you think of that?"

Dana didn't answer. She hadn't heard. She sat with her chin cupped in one hand and blinked slowly.

Her mother kept sorting. Dana watched her for a few minutes.

"Mom," she asked finally, "why do you bother with all this stuff? It's junk."

Her mother looked at her for a moment, then back down at the piles of cloth on the table. "You know, honey," she said, "you'd be surprised at how much worth these things still have left in them. We throw things away so easily because we only look at what's worn out or not working and forget about what's left. I like to look at the good these clothes still have in them and the good that can be done because of them."

"Huh?"

"Dana, it's like a ripple effect. Sorting these clothes keeps bags and bags of stuff out of the land-fill. That's a good thing in itself. It also gives groups of quilters something to do and other people to be with on quilting days. A lot of those people are lonely. Many of them don't go out much otherwise, and the quilt-making days are such a highlight for them. For some, their eyes aren't so good anymore, or their hands shake too much to sew. But they come and sort squares or give advice on colors. And they are just as proud as all the others when the project is done. The quilts turn out so beautifully. Sometimes they are sold and the money is used for a good cause. Sometimes they are given away to young mothers or to homeless shelters. Either way, someone benefits. Someone gets to be warm at night and to know others thought of them, and it's all because of bags of old clothes."

Dana thought for a moment. "But it's just so much work."

Her mother smiled. "Yes, it is. But it's always worth it to work hard for something you believe is important. Don't you think so?"

"I guess."

Her mother opened a new bag. "How's volley-ball going?"

"Fine."

"School?"

"Fine."

"I see you picked up *The Wizard of Oz*," said her mother. "Like it?"

"We're doing it for our school play."

"Wow. That's a big project. Are you going to try out for a part?"

"Do you think I'd make a good Dorothy?"

"I think you'd be good in any role, Dana."

"Even Dorothy?"

"Is there a reason you shouldn't try for that part?"

"No."

"It would be a lot of work, but you could do it." Her mom smiled. "Did your dad ever tell you he was in *The Wizard of Oz* when he was in high school? He was the Scarecrow."

"Dad?"

"You should ask him about it." She paused before asking the next question. "How's Janelle these days?"

Dana didn't answer. She stared at her glass of milk.

"Sometimes when something good or bad happens to one person, it can have an effect on a lot of other people. Like the ripples we were just talking about."

Dana reached across the table and pulled a piece of material from the pile. It was red and gold. One side was frayed, but the other was still in good shape. "This is pretty," she said.

Her mother smiled. "It is." She came around the table to where Dana sat and put an arm around her shoulders. Dana leaned in to the hug. Neither of them said a word. After a few minutes, her mom glanced at the clock. "Think you should try to get some sleep now?" she asked softly.

Dana nodded. She rinsed her glass, left it in the sink and went back upstairs.

She punched up her pillows and pulled her blankets up to her chin. She stared at the ceiling. Part of her wanted to throw out her friendship with Janelle. Let it go. Did it have anything good left in it? Anything worth saving? Nothing had been the same since the accident.

She thought about having to turn to the very back page of the school newspaper last month to find a picture of her cross-country team while the big story about Janelle's accident filled the whole front page. About how the same thing had happened with the volleyball story and the article about the bracelets. She thought about being the only grade-six girl on the volleyball team. And the only grade-six girl not in the bracelet club. She thought about the first time she had met Janelle and how Janelle had told Mickey to stop teasing her friend. She thought about birthday parties and phone calls and sleepovers where they had giggled long into the night. She remembered trips to the library, to the pool, to the ice rink or for ice cream. She remembered the projects they had done together. Grasshoppers. The Great Horned Owl. Dreaming up Adventure Island.

Then she thought about the tropical-rain-forest project. She thought about Jason waiting by the gym, and a hard lump formed in her throat.

Julia had called her selfish and accused her of taking things away from Janelle. Then why did she feel so empty? Fixing things up with Janelle would be a lot of work. But was it worth it? And even if she thought so, what did Janelle think? Dana closed her eyes and rolled over onto her side, but she couldn't get comfortable. It was the pigtails. She pulled out the ribbons. That was another thing. What on earth was she going to do about the play?

Dana finally fell asleep. When she woke up, her mother had already left for a shift at the clinic. Her dad and Dale were emptying out the backyard composter. Dana pulled a box of cereal and a bowl out of the cupboard and brought them to the table. Resting against the back of her chair was a small pillow covered with the red-and-gold fabric. Dana smiled. She had an idea. If she couldn't have things back the way they were before, maybe she could try to recycle them and make them into something new. She thought about this while she ate breakfast. She thought some more while she made her bed and laid the pretty red-and-gold pillow on top of it. She was still thinking while she brushed her teeth and hair. Laying down the brush, she stared hard at herself in the mirror. Suddenly, she knew exactly what she should do. She had her regular Saturday chores to do, and then she was going to finish watching that DVD.

Seventeen

ON MONDAY MORNING Mr. B. led everyone to the auditorium. Anyone who wanted to be part of the crew was asked to write his or her name, along with a job title, on a piece of paper. Anyone who wanted to try out for the cast was asked to sit in the front row. Dana scanned the chairs. Just as she'd hoped, there was an empty one beside Janelle. She was chatting with Gina. Dana took a deep breath and walked over.

Before Dana could even sit down, Julia was there. "What are you doing?" she asked.

"I was just going to sit here, beside Nel— beside Janelle."

"But that's my seat. I was saving it. See, I left my sweater on it."

Dana saw a light-blue sweater hung over the back of the chair. "Oh." She backed away. "Sorry."

"So you *are* trying out for the part then?" Julia asked.

"Yes, well, I—"

"Good luck. I still think Janelle's got it though."

"Are you trying out too?"

"I have a role in mind. But I'm mostly here for moral support. For Janelle." Julia smiled quickly and then sat down. Dana looked for another empty seat in the front row. The only one open was on the end, next to Mickey. So far things were not going according to plan.

"Dana?" called Mr. B. Apparently, sitting on the end also meant she had to go first. She plodded up the steps to the stage.

The tryouts did not turn out to be at all what Dana had expected. She had practiced several lines from the play, but she wasn't asked to say any of them. Instead, Mr. B. handed Dana a slip of paper with four lines on it. *Mary had a little lamb/Little lamb, little lamb/Mary had a little lamb/Its fleece was white as snow.* He asked her to read them in a loud, clear voice. She did, although she felt a little silly.

"Thank you, Dana," said Mr. Bartholomew. "Stay put up there a minute, if you would. Now, here's how the auditions will go. Dana, be our guinea pig, would you? Read those lines again, but this time say them like you think a cowboy would."

A cowboy? Why would a cowboy say the lines to a preschool rhyme? Dana looked out at her classmates. Everyone was waiting for her to do something. So Dana pretended to pull down her hat, slipped her thumbs in the belt loops of her jeans and said the lines in a deep, slow voice.

"Excellent. That's the idea. Now, how do you think a three-year-old would say them?" asked Mr. B.

A three-year-old? Was he serious? She thought about her little cousin, Lily, who had come over with Uncle Paul and Aunt Darlene for Thanksgiving. Dana turned all the *l*'s and *r*'s into *w*'s. Using a high, singsongy voice, she tried again.

"Mawy had a wittle wamb, wittle wamb, wittle wamb. Mawy had a wittle wamb, its fweece was white as snow." Not knowing exactly what to do when she was finished, Dana stuck her thumb in her mouth, and everyone laughed and clapped. She felt her cheeks start to heat up, but Mr. B. grinned and thanked her and told her that was all. She could sit down.

Mickey was next. He had to read the same lines, first with a British accent, then with a southern drawl.

"How might a gorilla say them?" Mr. B. asked Amber.

"What about if you were a spy, Allie?"

Everyone laughed at Jason's dinosaur delivery. He stomped and roared, and his eyes were wide and a little wild.

"Trey, pretend you're a king," said Mr. B.

"Can you be a rock star, Neta?" he asked.

"You're an alien from outer space, Gina."

"Say them as if you were ninety," Mr. Bartholomew told Janelle. Her eyes lit up, and she hunched over and quivered and quavered her way through the four lines.

And finally, "How about a mad scientist, Julia?"

"Me? Oh no, I'm really just here to—"

"Give it a try," coaxed Mr. B.

Mr. Bartholomew had everyone say the same four lines but never the same way. He never asked anyone to say them as if they were Dorothy or a Wicked Witch or a Cowardly Lion. It was ridiculous. It was also fun. Dana had almost completely let go of her fear of playing a part. She'd forgotten about the Dorothy dilemma altogether.

"Thanks, everyone," said Mr. B. when they'd all had a turn. "That was terrific. I'll let everyone know tomorrow which part they'll have, but I already know I'm going to have a terrible time deciding who will play the lead. There are two of you who would be perfect."

Two? Dana stopped smiling. *Oh boy.*

Eighteen

"DANA!" AVERY AND Allie ran over to her at the bike racks the next morning. "Do you think Mr. B. will pick you to be Dorothy?"

"Well, I…" Dana unbuckled her helmet.

"Or do you think it will be Janelle? You both want that part, right? Do you think you'll get it?"

Before Dana could answer, the twins were gone. They had seen Janelle get out of her parents' car and raced over to her. Dana knew they were asking her the same questions. Either way, it was out of her hands now.

When Dana got into the classroom, there was a message on the board telling the class to head straight to the auditorium. Kids clustered in small groups, talking and laughing. Excitement hummed in the big room. Dana sat down at the same empty seat in the front row and waited. As the second bell sounded, Mr. Bartholomew jogged in, clapped his hands and jumped up on the stage. He grabbed a low stool for himself and asked everyone else to come up and sit in a circle.

"Well," he began when everyone was ready. "I'm really excited to be working on this project with such a talented bunch. This production is going to be excellent. It's going to be a lot of work, but if we do it right, it's not going to feel like a lot of work at all. Thank you to all of you who signed up to be the crew. You're every bit as important as the actors, and I'm not just saying that. We'll be counting on you to make everything look and sound spectacular. I've written out your jobs on these sheets. You can have a look at them in a few moments, but first, let's meet our cast. Let's begin with who will play Dorothy."

Dana tensed.

"This role—" Mr. B. didn't get far before Julia cut in. She jumped to her feet, unable to contain herself one second longer.

"Mr. B., we all know you have to choose between Janelle and Dana to play the part of Dorothy. But please—it's obvious, isn't it? You just have to give the role to Janelle. You simply have to. Because of all Janelle has been through. And because Dana still has sports and everything else, and Janelle doesn't."

It was very quiet. Julia sat down. Dana knew everyone was looking at her. She looked at the floor. She bit her lip, hard. She didn't want to be angry, but she was. She wasn't the one who had broken her leg over the summer. It seemed she was going to be punished for that all year long.

Mr. B. smiled. He nodded. "We all know Janelle has been through a great deal," he said.

Dana took a deep breath and drew in her shoulders. She tried to steel herself for what she knew was coming.

"We also know she had a great audition and that she would do a wonderful—"

Janelle cut in.

"Mr. B." She stood up, though it took her a second to get her balance. "Mr. B., I can't take the lead role."

"What?" cried Julia. "Why not? Is it too much for you? I can help!"

Janelle shook her head. "First of all," she said, "Dorothy needs to be able to skip and dance. Not limp around like I do."

Julia jumped in again. "We'll pretend she twists her ankle in the tornado!"

Janelle laughed. "That's very creative," she continued, "but secondly, and more important, I can't take the part because of Dana."

"Dana? Why? What has she done now?" Julia's lips were set in a thin, straight line.

"No, Julia, that's not what I mean." Janelle looked around the circle. "I want to thank you, so many of you, for everything you've done for me these last few months. You've helped me in all kinds of different ways, and I'm very grateful for all your support. But this is really very simple. The lead role should go to Dana because she would be great in it. She's very talented, and she's a very special person. She deserves it."

Janelle sat down. Julia had a puzzled look on her face. Dana's heart missed a beat. She let out a huge breath and looked up.

Everyone was quiet. They all looked at Dana, then back at Janelle. "Oh, and Mr. B., I need to tell you one more thing," said Janelle. "I don't know if it makes a difference, but the part I really wanted was the—"

"Wicked Witch?" asked the teacher.

Janelle looked surprised. She smiled. "Yes, I think my limp will work perfectly with that role."

Mr. B. laughed. "I'm sure it will add to it wonderfully, Janelle, but limp or no limp, I already had you pegged for that role the first time I heard you cackle."

Dana looked up. "That was you?"

"Who else?" said Janelle. She cackled wickedly. The whole class laughed and applauded.

When it quieted down again, everyone looked at Dana. "But Janelle," she asked slowly, "Dorothy? Me? Do you really think so? What about my..." She hesitated. She cleared her throat. "What about my hair?"

"What about your hair? There's a wig, of course."

"Oh." *Of course. Why hadn't she thought of that?* Dana stood up. "Okay, I think it's great that some of you think I can play the lead role." She stole a look at Jason. He was busy stuffing his shoelaces inside his shoes and didn't look up. "But, even if it sounds weird, I need to tell you that the part I really wanted was the—"

"Scarecrow?" asked Mr. B.

Dana nodded. She smiled. "Yes, the Scarecrow."

Julia looked even more puzzled.

"That's exactly what I thought. You'd be perfect for that part, Dana. It's yours."

Dana sat down. Everyone applauded. She felt her cheeks get hot.

"Jason," continued Mr. Bartholomew, "I have you as the Tin Man."

Oh. Dana felt her cheeks getting hotter still. *The Tin Man? The Tin Man needed a heart. Jason needed a heart. A heart that had room in it for more than kickball. This was perfect. It couldn't get any better if Dana had chosen the parts herself.*

"And Mickey," said Mr. B., "you're the Lion."

Oh well.

Mr. B. waved the papers he had in each hand. "I have a list here for everyone who will play the Munchkins, and a list here for everyone who will be a Flying Monkey. Allie, you're Auntie Em. Trey, you're the Wizard. Let's put that great voice of yours to work. Amber, I've chosen you to be the Good Witch. You've got such a lovely smile, we want to see you use it!"

That Mr. B. He saw the potential in everyone.

He went on for a few more minutes. "Well, class," Mr. Bartholomew said at last, "that's everyone, I think. We're off to see the Wizard, the Wonderful Wizard of—"

"No, wait," piped up Julia, shaking her head. "Mr. B., if you didn't choose Janelle or Dana to be Dorothy…" She looked around. "Who did you pick?"

"Ahhh, of course. Dorothy. I almost forgot." He slapped his forehead and smiled. "Well, Julia, you'll remember I said I had a difficult time choosing between two people?" She nodded. "One of them was you."

"Me?" Everyone was stunned. Even Julia seemed surprised.

"You would be fantastic."

"I would?"

"She would?" asked Mickey. Allie poked him.

"Of course she would," said Janelle. She started to clap, and soon everyone joined in.

Julia looked confused. She held her hands up, asking for quiet. "Wait. Wait." She put her hands on her hips. "But Mr. B.," she said, "don't you need me to be the director? I didn't see that role on the crew list, but I assumed that was because, well…" She looked around. "Isn't it obvious?"

Mr. Bartholomew laughed—a big, booming laugh. "You know, Julia," he said, "I was going to do that job myself, but if you would be willing to take it on, that would be excellent. Thank you for offering." He paused. "Well, then, let me introduce Dorothy, everyone. Neta?"

Neta looked like she'd swallowed the script.

"Me?"

"You."

"Dorothy?"

"Of course."

Neta rose to her feet uncertainly.

"Take notice, everyone. This girl can sing!" said Mr. B.

The shoes! The blue-and-white shoes! "That was you?" Dana asked. "In the bathroom? Singing?"

Neta blushed. "The acoustics are good in there."

Dana sighed with relief. Everyone else jumped to their feet and cheered.

Nineteen

THE STUDENTS SCATTERED, looking at lists, talking about the play and their roles in it. Jason and Mickey were already telling the costume crew what they had in mind for the Tin Man and the Lion.

"Everyone," called out a grinning Mr. B. after a moment, waving his hands to get the class's attention, "listen up, please. There's one more cast member I want you to meet. Have a seat for a minute, and I'll bring him right in."

Mr. B. disappeared backstage while the students sat down again.

"Who do you think he means?" asked Neta.

"Not a clue," said Dana. "But I think we're about to find out."

Mr. B. came back in carrying a box. "Class," he announced, "I'd like you to meet Bitsy. My sister, who lives close to the school, has generously agreed to let her little dog play the part of Toto in our production."

A bad feeling descended on Dana. A little dog? Close to the school? No, she thought, it couldn't be. But it was. Buddy! The little dog peeked over the side of the box, looked around at everyone and gave a sharp little bark. Then he jumped out and ran straight to Neta.

"Look out!" Dana warned. But Bitsy didn't bite or growl. Instead, he jumped up and began licking Neta's face furiously.

"Look at that," said Mr. B., chuckling. "It seems you're friends already."

"Oh, Dana, look," said Neta. "Isn't he sweet? Isn't he just the cutest? Here, do you want to hold him?"

"No! Uh, that is, we've met before, and I don't think Bitsy likes me." Bitsy jumped over into Dana's lap and began licking her face.

Neta looked at Dana, eyebrows raised. "Sure it wasn't some sort of misunderstanding?"

Mr. B. reached out for Bitsy and held the squirming pup in one arm. "Well," he said, rubbing the little dog behind the ears, "as long as we don't put any of our cast members on bicycles, I think things will work out fine. My sister did warn me that Bitsy has a thing about moving bikes."

Bikes? Dana rolled her eyes and smiled.

Everyone crowded around to see Bitsy.

Julia appeared beside Dana. She already had a pen and paper in her hand. Tomorrow, thought Dana, she'd probably come wearing a beret and snapping one of those "Take 2" signs.

"Well," said Julia, "parts for everyone, and Toto too."

Dana laughed. "He seems to like Neta. I think she'll make a great Dorothy."

Julia nodded. "Yes. She's probably good with dogs too. She has two of them, and her mom is a veterinarian."

"I didn't know that," said Dana. She wondered what else she didn't know about Neta. She thought maybe she'd like to get to know her better.

"Cast meeting tomorrow," said Julia. "Here's a reminder." She scribbled out the message and peeled the piece of paper off for Dana.

Dana stared at the paper. She felt a strange, prickly sensation all over.

"Is there a problem with meeting tomorrow?" asked Julia.

"What? No." She shook her head. "Julia, you have frog-shaped sticky notes?"

"I wish. Aren't they the greatest? They're Janelle's. You're sure you can make it tomorrow?"

Dana took the note and nodded. "Sure," she said.

She looked at the paper. Janelle's. Of course. They always chose the same things. Dana tucked the note into her pocket. Sure, she could make the meeting tomorrow. But there was something else she needed to do today.

Dana looked for Janelle. She saw her sitting against the back wall of the stage. She had her head back and eyes closed, with her legs stretched out straight in front of her. Dana walked over and sat down beside her. She didn't say anything.

Neither did Janelle. For a long moment, it was quiet between them. From the back of the room, Trey belted out, "I am the great and powerful Oz," and both girls jumped.

"Pay no attention to the man behind the curtain," said Dana.

Janelle smiled, but she didn't look her way.

After a moment, Dana tried again. "Thanks for saying what you said, about me playing Dorothy."

"It's true. You would have done a great job. Just like you'll do with the Scarecrow." Janelle still did not look at her.

Dana took a deep breath. She had so much she wanted to say, but she was afraid. She heard her mother's voice telling her, "You can recycle that!" and she knew it was true. But where would she start? At the beginning, she decided.

"I'm sorry I didn't come to see you in the hospital," she said, staring straight ahead.

"I know you don't like hospitals." Janelle said. Then she added softly, "But I wish you had."

"Me too."

It was quiet again.

"I was sad you were in there," said Dana.

Janelle nodded. "Me too."

"I'm sorry I wasn't there for you."

Janelle sighed. "And I'm sorry I wasn't there for you."

Dana looked at her. "What do you mean?"

"This summer…working, soccer, just hanging out. And this fall…running and volleyball."

"But you couldn't—"

"I know. But I'm still sorry you had to do it by yourself. That must have been kind of lonely for you. We were going to do it together. I let you down."

That was it, Dana thought—the empty feeling. It was loneliness.

There was silence for a moment. Dana shook her head. "You didn't let me down." Then she said quietly, "I thought I'd lost you."

"Never," answered Janelle.

"First the accident, and then…" She paused. She felt her cheeks redden.

Janelle turned to look at Dana. "Then?" she asked.

"I thought you were mad at me. I thought that you thought I was taking everything away from you." She hesitated.

"Go on."

"Meanwhile, I felt you were trying to take everything away from me. That if you couldn't have them, I shouldn't have them either. Running, volleyball…I even thought you might be trying to meet with Jason behind my back."

"What?" Janelle's eyes widened. "And I thought you were avoiding me because you thought I wasn't cool enough to be your friend anymore."

"Cool enough? You're the best! I thought you didn't need me anymore," said Dana. "I thought you and Julia…"

"Ah, Julia."

They both looked over at Julia, who was talking with Neta as she handed her a piece of green paper. "Julia, well, she's a take-charge kind of person," said Janelle. "I guess I was her project for a while, but I think she may have a new one now. She means well, you know. She really does."

She looked back at Dana. "But no one could ever replace you, Dana. I missed you."

Dana closed her eyes and took a deep breath. "I missed you too. I know things will have to be different, but that's okay. We can make it work. I'll have to finish out the volleyball season, but I won't sign up for basketball."

"What are you talking about? Of course you will. Just look at how tall you are—you'll be dangerous out there! You'll be the team's secret weapon. No fair that you get to be tall and have curly hair too. Everyone's jealous."

Jealous? Dana opened her mouth to reply, but no words came out.

"Maybe I can help keep score or something," continued Janelle. "Anyway, I'll come to all the games."

Dana gave her head a shake. "Awesome," she said, "and you can come over and we'll practice the lines of the play together. I have this great dance I want to show you that would be perfect for the Scarecrow. Mr. Finch taught us."

"Mr. Finch? This I've got to see. Show me now."

Dana laughed as they stood up. "Oh, Nelly—" she started, but then she stopped, flustered. "Oops, sorry, I mean…"

"Why *oops*?"

"You said you didn't like to be called kindergarten names anymore."

"But you always call me Nelly."

"Yeah, but…"

A lightbulb went on for Janelle. "Oh, that. I thought you were talking about what Mickey used to call me. Remember?"

Dana shook her head.

"Jelly Belly. Remember? *Jelly Belly, she's so smelly*. He used to say it all the time." Janelle paused and put her hands on her hips. "Wait a minute. He used to call you something too, didn't he?"

Dana shook her head again.

"Yes, he did. What was it?"

Dana put her hands over her ears. She knew what was coming.

"Jelly Belly and…Ding Dong! That's it. *Ding Dong Davis. Sing a song, Ding Dong.* I remember now. Only Mickey was the one doing all the singing. Yes, that was it. Ding Dong Davis."

"Shhh," said Dana. "Not so loud!" They grinned at each other. It felt good to be grinning with her friend again.

Right on cue, Mickey came toward them, singing, "*If I were King of the Forrressttt…*"

"Maybe he'll learn a whole new set of songs now," whispered Janelle as Mickey got closer. "No more Dana, Dana tunes."

Dana raised an eyebrow. "Think so?"

Mickey stopped right in front of them. "So you're the Witch," he said to Janelle. "The Wicked Witch."

Janelle nodded. "Looks like it."

"And you're the Scarecrow?" he asked Dana.

Dana nodded. "Guess so."

Mickey nodded too. "This is going to be fun," he said as he began to walk away. "Jay's pretty pumped too. He's excited about being partners."

"With you?"

"Well, yeah. But even more about being partners with you, if you know what I mean." He winked.

Dana blushed. Janelle grinned.

"Hey," said Mickey. "Your face is as red as a—"

Don't say tomato! But Mickey just turned and started singing again. "Scarecrow Dana, if she only had a brain-a."

Dana rolled her eyes. "I suppose he means well too?"

"He really does," said Janelle.

Dana smiled.

"Come on," begged Janelle. "Show me that Scarecrow dance you were talking about." She leaned in and whispered, "While we're practicing it at your house, we can talk about what kind of spell we'll cast on the Tin Man." She cackled softly.

"I was thinking we might invite Neta too," said Dana. "If that's okay with you."

"Sure. I'd like to get to know her better. And she's going to need help with all those lines."

"Okay, do what I do," Dana said. She flapped her arms wildly and shook her head until her cheeks jiggled. Janelle joined in. They started laughing. They laughed so hard they almost couldn't stand anymore and had to hold each other up. They laughed so hard, tears began pooling in the corners of their eyes. Some of the other kids looked over and started laughing too, until the whole auditorium echoed with laughter. It was a ripple effect.

Acknowledgments

SPECIAL THANKS TO my husband and family for their enthusiasm and constant encouragement. Sincere thanks also to Amy Collins and the many others at Orca Books who are so lovely to work with and do their jobs so well.

SYLVIA TAEKEMA works as a supply teacher and as a volunteer in programs for children at school, church and in the community. Her first novel, *Seconds*, was nominated for a Silver Birch Express Award. Sylvia lives in Chatham, Ontario, where she loves to read, bake cookies and go on camping adventures with her family.